ANCIENT PORCELAIN

Behind Blue Eyes: Book 5

SARA J. BERNHARDT

Lavish
Publishing LLC

First Edition

Behind Blue Eyes, book 5

2020 Lavish Publishing, LLC - Midland

All Rights Reserved

Published in the United States by Lavish Publishing, LLC, Midland, TX

Cover Design by: Alexcia Productions

Cover Images: CANSTOCK

Paperback Edition

ISBN- 978-1-64900-006-4

www.LavishPublishing.com

Contents

"Do you not think that there are things which you cannot understand, and yet which are; that some people see things that others cannot? But there are things old and new which must not be contemplate by men´s eyes, because they know -or think they know- some things which other men have told them. Ah, it is the fault of our science that it wants to explain all; and if it explain not, then it says there is nothing to explain."

— Bram Stoker, Dracula

For My Adam

Prologue

SINCE ADAM HAD LEFT ME, I hadn't wanted to speak with Verarsoe. But who better to be with than Verarsoe, my maker? So powerful that nobody dared question him. Of course, except for Adam—and I must say, the outcomes of that were most unpleasant.

I went to the chapel to find Adam. There were many rumors and gossip around the vampire community. I was, at first, overjoyed that Adam had returned, but seeing him in such a state was devastating. Would he ever be the same again? Would he ever want me back?

A slight sense of panic almost paralyzed me for a moment; I took a deep breath and closed my tense brown eyes. *He had to return, didn't he?*

As my eyes remained closed, I felt for a scent, hunted for a familiar presence. All I felt was Adam, sitting there on the floor below me, hands clasped together to the point where his knuckles turned whiter than his already pale skin. He didn't know I was there; I would come here often now to see him in his mysterious trance, searching for only a glimmer of awareness or life in him. I feared that soon, he would waste away before that cross, trying to beg forgiveness for sins he would commit over and over again, and he would never return to claim his wealth or estate. He looked very human, sitting there as if he were lost in his very own dreams—perhaps he was. Tears ran down his cheeks and lay in the crevices of his lips, resting between them; still— he did not move. If not for the blood running from his eyes, I may have supposed him asleep. If not for the visible hardness of his flesh, I *would* have supposed him human—but he was neither.

My thoughts of Adam were in an instant shattered by a very familiar feeling, the presence I had been half expecting every evening I came to this old church. I never actually thought I would find him, but the tingling in my body—the tremor in the atmosphere—this confirmed it. At last, he had come back to me. I tried not to let my emotion show.

I felt a hand on my shoulder, or I thought it was a hand; it was something cold and hard, like metal or stone perhaps. I knew it was he. The presence didn't startle me. I turned and stared hard into his face.

"At last," he whispered, but he didn't touch me, not except for the hand on my shoulder.

"How did you find me?" I whispered.

"You are my child. I know always where to find you."

"So, you have returned to me, Master?"

"Ah, Relone. It is time we become each other's again. Will you let me know you again? Can you tell me?" he asked in a kind manner, smiling thinly.

I realized then how much I had missed him, and it startled me.

"If I promise," he started, "not to press my opinions of your darling Adam upon you, if I promise not to press you at all…" He trailed off.

I could hear the desperation in his voice. "In time, Master."

Verarsoe was gone now. I smiled faintly.

"Still the same," I whispered to myself. "Some things never change—like us."

I stared again at that beautiful fiend below me. So good, with a soul meant for evil. How he must be struggling —suffering.

I couldn't feel the presence of my master any longer, but there was a kind of comfort in my loneliness. What is *my* eternal purpose? If I had an eternal purpose as Adam, wouldn't I be here too as Adam? In the church for months unmoving?

It's been over two hundred years since he left me. Even Rayne had not heard from him. I knew in my bones where he dwelled—in the ground, sleeping away the centuries.

Many come here to this church to see the legendary Adam Gold, just to see if he is real, but he looked weak, vulnerable. Not the Adam they thought they knew, not the beauty they thought they were looking for.

My eyes were opened by another presence, one that slightly disturbed me. I looked in that direction. Could it be? Somebody had followed me here. My mind had been open. Had he been reading my thoughts? I looked at him, then immediately turned away, staring straightforward to the cracked, stained glass window across the way.

"Why did you come?" I whispered.

"Why wouldn't I come?"

"Leave me," I snapped. "You have no right to be here."

It was only Victor who stood there beside me. I refused to make eye contact. I didn't like him. His light hair shone beautifully in the glimmer of the night's light, his auburn eyes staring from beneath his blond eyebrows.

"I have just as much a right to be here as you," he said. "How is he?"

"Look at him," I spat. "How does he look?"

"Like a coward."

I scoffed and turned to face him. "What do you want?"

"Just you."

"What are you saying?"

"All the time we spent together, you never told me, Relone."

"Told you what?"

He smiled. "Your story. You never told me your story."

"I do not wish to now, either."

"I think you do," he said with a smile in his words. "I think you want someone to know you."

He *had* read me. I sighed, unable to argue now. "Are you certain you wish to hear such a long tale?"

"Yes," he replied without hesitation, "I am."

I LED Victor to the old rundown apartment buildings, just blocks from the Harmony Grave Cemetery near Jefferson Avenue.

"We have time," I said. "Dawn is far. We have hours."

"Hours it is," he said with a smile.

Yes, hours this tale would take, many long hours.

"I'm not as I used to be," I told him. "I'm something of a new person now, Victor." I felt him tense at the preternatural sound of my voice and had to force myself not to smile.

"We all change…whether we mean to or not. Nobody can stay the same forever."

I nodded. "Yes, I suppose that's true."

"Where does your story begin?"

"Paris. My story begins in Paris. Here is where you would find scholars and many works from the greatest philosophers of all time. Here, you may find Aristotle, Socrates, and more.

"By my thirteenth year of age, it was the year 1310, which was a time when the reign of law was being extended. It was three years after The Order of the Templars had been passed. Paris was a city feverish with new ideas, art, and music.

"The artist, Victor Hugo, described Paris as a dark, violent, and pathetic place—the way it appeared to him from his tower in Notre Dame. Of course, Paris was not at all as he thought. Even in those times, it was the greatest city in the world. There were some artists who portrayed my beautiful city in the right way, such as Michelangelo and Charles Peguy. It was described as a paradise, and it truly was."

Chapter One

I DON'T REMEMBER a lot about my childhood, just that I was always alone. I didn't really know what home was. My mother and father had both left me. I'm guessing now that they had died when I was very small.

It's been over five hundred years, and I can still hear the bell towers, can still smell my master's cooking, can feel Sophia's touch. It's been over five centuries, and I can still recall the love I had for my master—my master, Verarsoe.

I was always alone during the day. I didn't know where it was that he went, but Lord how I hated being alone! I hated it more than anything in this world!

He came to me late one night and spoke to me softly. I will spare you the old language of the times.

"You know you are my child," he said. "I do not leave during the day to hurt you. You are my beloved."

"I love you, Master."

He smiled, and I remember loving that more than anything. His smile meant so many different things, and it was unlike any other I had seen. There was something about the way his teeth were pointed like those of a wolf. There was something about the way his skin was always hard like metal. It didn't frighten me, though perhaps it should have.

He taught me to read and write. He taught me about my home, France.

My learning was slow at first, I must admit, but my master was never harsh with me. I truly hated to disappoint him, and sometimes when I saw it in his eyes, it would make me weep. On rare occasions, before he left for the night, he let me sleep in his bed so I could feel closer to him.

I waited through the days, waiting for dusk when I could be with my master for the few precious hours before I slept.

Verarsoe loved to read and would read to me often when I was young. He recited books of poetry and stories from the Bible. I know I had a sister, though many of my early memories of her are vague. She was with my master before me. Though she was called my sister, truly, she was not. She didn't hate me for the way I clung to my master or the way I ran to his embrace every evening. She was kind.

Her name was Sophia. She had black hair always piled upon her head and coal-black eyes.

I don't know how it came to be that she was in France with my master when she was a lovely Spanish girl. I didn't question it at the time. I accepted that my master was a sort of wizard. Sophia spoke perfect French and kept me company during the days. We would play games to pass the time. Those memories are some of my happiest.

The candles were lit by the servants one evening, and I ached for the arrival of Verarsoe. Sometimes I would fall into a panic, terrified he would not come home. That never did happen, though sometimes he was very late. I never asked him about it. I was sure he would not tell me even if I were to ask. He was very secretive about his business during the day.

"Do not worry, dark eyes," he whispered to me. "I will always be here in the dark hours."

He was true to his word. He was always there to put me to bed, and when he was late, the house was run the same.

The days seemed so long without him, but Sophia kept me company and played the violin for me and sang songs in Spanish. Her voice was like silver, or something liquid. The lyrics rolled off her tongue and dripped from her soft lips. Though I didn't understand the words, her music always brought me peace. She took care of me as a big sister would. She was only a few years older than me and seemed very content with the life she had. I loved her, of course, but Verarsoe was all I thought about. I longed to understand him, to know his secrets.

I would often go exploring through the house, even into my master's study, where I was not allowed. There was one evening when a young maid had caught me rifling through Verarsoe's compositions. She ducked away and left the room.

I was anxious about my master's return that night. I was sure he would whip me when he found out. When he came to me, he scolded me, and when I cried, he lifted me in his arms and carried me to bed.

"You have not been keeping up with your studies," he said.

"I do not want to learn those things, Master. I want to learn about you. I want to know your secrets."

He could move with speed no man could master, had the strength of twenty men, could hear my words before I spoke them, and I wanted to learn to do the same.

"In time," he said. "When you are ready. You keep out of my study, or I will take pleasure in whipping you."

I shuddered, knowing he meant it.

Chapter Two

ABOUT TWO YEARS passed before I had finally mastered the art of literature, and at last, I could speak Latin and Italian. I understood the Bible along with the art and literature of my time. Sophia learned along with me, but Verarsoe seemed to hardly notice her.

I always wondered, if he were so powerful, why he didn't have packs of boys flocking to his doors, crying out for his magic. I wasn't bothered by that, of course. It meant there was no competition for his affection.

The first clear memory I have of Sophia isn't until a year later. I awoke alone, the same as every morning. I remember feeling more alone than usual, and I wept for my master. Sophia came in to comfort me like she often did.

"He'll be here," she said in perfect French.

I tried to smile.

She left the room and came back with her violin. It always cheered me up when she played her lovely Spanish melodies.

I thanked her for her kindness, and she sat beside me on the edge of my bed. She looked so beautiful, so delicate. I pulled the pin from her piled hair, letting the thick curls fall loose around her shoulders. She smiled, not moving to stop me.

Perhaps it was because she was so different than most of the women—the maids—I was acquainted with that I was so drawn to her; perhaps it was because she was Spanish and I was not used to girls that looked brown-skinned and black-eyed, or perhaps it was something more than that.

Her little white dress covered so much of her. I wished I could just rip it off to see her in all her beauty unmasked. She stared at me, smiling, but her smile slowly faded as she squinted her eyes to stare into mine. She slid the strands of my gray hair through her pretty brown fingers and moved them behind my ear.

"Your eyes are tense," she said. "Why?"

I didn't respond.

She whispered something in Spanish, but to this day, I don't know what she said.

"You're trembling, Relone," she whispered. "Are you all right?"

I nodded, unsure how to respond. I still wasn't used to speaking to her.

She leaned forward. I felt my heart rate speed up. The warmth of her spread through me, and the softness of her lips pressed gently against my cheek. I closed my eyes, savoring the feeling, but it wasn't enough. There was a need within me, a longing for her I had never felt until this moment. I pulled her close and kissed her lips. She returned the affection without hesitation. It happened so fast without any warning, but it felt too good to question, too right. It was as if all the lights came on and I realized why I was alive. She was meant for me.

Her white gown lay strewn across the floor, and the pearls had fallen from her neck onto the pillow. I squeezed them in my hand for a moment before throwing them to the floor with her discarded dress.

She felt so small and delicate beneath me, and I feared I was hurting her. I could feel the press of her tiny rounded belly upon my own, her hard breathing upon my face, her heart pounding, her body trembling, and it frightened me. I didn't want to hurt her; I didn't want to hurt anybody.

My thoughts immediately took a violent turn, and I remembered my master. He would have never approved of this, and he would know. He always knew. Without me saying a word, he always knew everything. What would he do to me for this? I sprang away from her without warning.

She whispered my name, but I couldn't look at her. I felt her kiss my shoulder.

"It's all right," she said.

"Did I…did I hurt you?"

"Of course not," she whispered, leaning against me.

I turned to her, and she was smiling, covering her beauty with the sheets of the bed.

"You're beautiful…so beautiful."

THOUGH WE NEVER SPOKE OF that afternoon again, I was sure my master knew. He never mentioned it to me, but he looked at me differently.

I knew my master was preparing to leave me again as he always did. I wanted to say something—anything to get him to stay. Even if it was to scold me—even beat me.

"Your wine is delicious," I said.

An angry expression flickered across his face, but it vanished as soon as it appeared. "Fool of a boy."

"I would not say I am a boy any longer, Master."

His eyes tensed in an unnatural way. "You are still a boy."

"Only because you want me to be."

"Do you dare question me?"

I could finally hear the anger in his voice, and I knew I

was getting to him. I could feel the anxiety creeping into my chest, but I wasn't going to give in. "Yes, Master, I do."

He took one long stride toward me. Every instinct told me to fall back, but I held my ground.

"Master—yes," he said, pointing an angry finger at my chest. "How dare you."

"Maybe you shouldn't be. You leave me here all alone. You are cruel. You should not be my master at all."

His features tensed again, and the anger in his eyes turned to fury. Without any hesitation, I felt the weight of his hand crash against my cheek. The stinging in my skin brought tears to my eyes, but I tried to hide it.

"Fiend," I grumbled, my eyes staring at him from the side, my hand covering my throbbing cheek. "Fiend."

"Master!" he yelled. "Would you rather me not be? Would you rather be on the streets, dying of hunger, thirst, disease?"

"Hit me."

"Why?"

"Because you will hit me anyway after I say this."

He didn't budge, but I knew he was waiting for me to speak.

The feelings poured out of me, and I found myself unable to stop. "Why do you leave me? I don't leave you. I never would. You are a monster, a fiend. You are cruel and cold to me, but at the same time, you say you love me, and you take care of me. Why can't you be the master you are supposed to be?"

He was silent for a moment, and it made me nervous.

"I will not hit you for that," he said. "But I should, and I should take pleasure in it too. I am the master that I should be. I teach you, clothe you, feed you. I protect you from the evils of the world. I am everything I should be. I will never cease to be, as long as you remain the pupil that you are supposed to be, and that includes obeying me."

Without another word, he left me. My sadness was now rekindled to anger. All I could think was if he could do this to me, leave, then why couldn't I do the same to him?

I ran to his bedchambers, ignoring the questioning glance from Sophia. His room was sparkling clean. Everything was in its proper place as it always was. I rummaged through his desk drawers, looking for money. I shuffled through the papers on his desk. Nothing.

On the bureau, I spotted a small wooden box. It was covered in delicate engravings of angels with big feathered wings. I ran my fingers over the wood, loving the softness. I continued glancing around the room until my eye caught a tiny key attached to a fancy gold tassel. I gripped the key between my fingers, enjoying the coolness. My heart rate quickened, and beads of sweat broke out on my forehead. My hands were shaking. I inhaled, trying in vain to ease my nerves. My master would beat me mercilessly for this—

possibly even kill me. But that only made me more determined—more excited.

I opened the box, and instantly a smile forced its way onto my face, and I almost laughed. I had found where my master hid his money, and I stuffed it into my pockets. Without even a word to Sophia, I left. I had no idea where I was going, so I just walked. I walked for a long time, ignoring the beggars in the gutters trying to sell me flowers or trinkets. The air turned frigid and chilled me to the bone. I pulled my cloak over my chest and dashed inside a tavern I was passing by.

The tavern was unlike anything I had ever experienced. Everywhere was noise and girls, people fighting and drinking. I sat on one of the empty barstools and immediately had multiple girls hanging on me, trying to get my attention.

After the first drink I had, my memory gets fuzzy. I knew Verarsoe would not approve, which only made me want to do it more. I relished in a new sense of freedom.

Chapter Three

HER NAME WAS Claudia La Croux. She had dark hair and eyes of cobalt blue. She wasn't pretty like Sophia, but I knew I would be going against my master, so I let her take me back to her home. There, she had wine. I discovered the pleasure in getting wildly drunk and the torment of getting violently sick.

I stayed with Claudia for three days. They were three days of drunken lovemaking and meaningless games. She taught me to gamble. We visited taverns and alleyways, drinking and gambling. I learned over those days that I liked to sing. I sang loud songs in French as if in celebration. I made people laugh, mostly because I did it after consuming copious amounts of alcohol.

Sometimes, I forgot entirely about Verarsoe. Other times, I missed him terribly. Although my obscene behavior amused everyone around me, it was no longer enough. I missed my master and Sophia. I missed the warmth, safety, and love I had back home. I knew it was time to return; I had known for a while. Every time I tried, I was halted by crippling fear of what my master would do to me. My mind flashed with images of broken skin and purple bruises covering my body from head to toe. I could see the lack of love in Verarsoe's eyes. My chest tightened with anxiety. He could kill me if he wanted to. And why wouldn't he at this point? All I wanted was to understand him, to have him love me as I loved him. I felt I had destroyed any chance I once had of finding what I was looking for.

My thoughts took a different turn then. What if he *did* kill me? What was I living for now? I needed him more than I wanted to admit, and my mind haunted me with memories of Sophia and the guilt I felt for betraying her. Even though we had never established what we were, I knew it was wrong to give myself to another.

My lovely companion thought I had fallen ill. I had stopped drinking and never touched her anymore. I awoke one morning with Claudia beside me in a silken nightdress.

I sat up, not remembering at first where I was. I sighed, still thinking about home.

"I'm sure I can put a smile on that grim face of yours." She laughed.

I smiled; I let her kiss me—I didn't care.

And as she lay beneath me, I remembered Sophia. I gasped and jumped from the bed, frantic now, scrambling for my clothes. I dressed myself, and without another word, I ran from the house. She called out to me, but I ignored. I ran quickly—sickened by what I had done.

I didn't go home yet, though; I returned to the tavern. I almost felt at home there, only because everybody knew me, and the girls loved me. They twisted my hair around their fingers and hung all about me as I continued to get drunker and drunker.

I reached into my pocket to glance at the pocket watch I had stolen along with my master's money and realized it was missing. I cursed silently to myself. I must have lost it sometime during my drunken haze with Claudia. I knew she would be back at the tavern, looking for me, but I couldn't even bear to look at her. I had to leave before she showed up.

I walked the streets before sunset on my way back home. I wouldn't miss Claudia at all; I wasn't expecting to. Perhaps I would miss the adoration from the others, but I wasn't expecting that either.

I walked slowly with my numb hands tucked under my crossed arms. It was very cold out, and it was getting dark.

I bowed my head against the wind that had picked up. I halted, my feet hitting against a pair of heavy boots. I looked up, meeting the tense dark eyes of a large man. His hair was jet black, and his short, pointed beard appeared unkempt and dirty.

I backed away, knowing something was not right.

"You are the child of Monsieur Mirior. Are you not?"

I choked on my breath. How could he have possibly known?

"Are you not?" he pressed, his face twisting into an expression of anger.

I didn't want to answer, but nor could I lie. He would know, and I was too frightened to risk it. "His—his ward," I stammered. "Yes."

He took another step toward me, his lips curling into a devilish grin. I realized I was dressed in my fine clothes, and it occurred to me that I was lucky this hadn't happened before now. I knew this was going to end badly. I silently called out to Verarsoe, wishing he were here to save me and deeply offended when he did not come. I didn't have any money left to offer the man, and I knew there was no way I could fight back, so I turned and ran. Before I had even reached the corner, I was on the ground with the robber's fists in my back and shoulders, his feet in my face.

I curled into a ball, trying to protect my head. I screamed and wept, calling out for my master. He never came to my aid. Nobody did.

Once the strikes ceased, I stayed on the ground, reeling in pain. I managed to slip my hand under my shirt and brush my fingers across my sore skin. I whimpered at the sight of blood on my fingertips.

It was already dark and still a while before I could get to my feet. I felt lucky then to even be alive. I feared if I didn't go home soon, something like this would happen again, though my clothes were now tarnished and torn, and my face was battered and bruised. Perhaps that was for the best, as I did not expect to be so lucky twice.

It was very cold as I made my way home. I tucked my numb hands under my arms again, trying to ignore the pain. As soon as I came to the door of the estate, a great comfort washed over me. I stepped inside, sighing in relief at the welcoming warmth, healing my frost-bitten fingers. The anxiety returned as I approached the door to my master's chambers. It was late, so I was sure he was there. When I opened the door, I saw he was sitting at his desk, writing furiously. He didn't turn to look at me, but I was sure he knew I was there. His face appeared tranquil, which put me slightly at ease. He kept his eyes on his writing, re-dipped his quill, and continued.

The pain in my body had not subsided, and without anything else to distract me, I was instantly fully aware of it. It was almost suffocating. My vision blurred, and dizziness took over. My muscles weakened and gave out. My chest tightened, and my stomach churned. I tried to ease my breathing and keep my footing but to no avail, and I crashed to the floor, unconscious.

WHEN I AWOKE, my head was still foggy, and it took me a few moments to remember where I was. I looked around, realizing I was in my bed, with Verarsoe standing near the door—a whip in hand. He took a long stride toward the bed, and I cowered, covering my face with my arms, prepared for the blow.

I cringed when I heard the deafening crack of the whip, but I felt no pain. I heard him chuckle quietly, and I looked up.

"It appears you have been punished enough, Relone."

I could feel him tearing the cloth of my already torn shirt, revealing my naked back. I winced from the pain.

"I have the healing liquid, dark eyes," he said softly. He pressed his palm to my lips, and a hot liquid flowed into my mouth. I could taste the salt of his skin and the metal of his blood. It rolled through my body like a ball of fire. My entire body tingled from the top of my head to the tips of my outstretched fingers.

When he pulled away, it was almost torturous.

"More," I whispered.

"Sleep now."

I tried to protest, tried to keep begging, but I was too tired, and I fell into a deep slumber.

I awoke later during the night in a panic, thinking my master would be gone. I shot up in bed, calling out to him.

"I'm here," I heard him say. "It's all right. I'm right here, my dark eyes."

I relaxed, feeling the comfort I always did in his presence. My body didn't ache anymore, and I glanced at my skin. No bruises, no cuts—nothing.

"You…healed me."

He nodded.

"With…with your blood."

He approached me, his expression unreadable. "It will all make sense to you, Relone…in time."

"Tell me where it is, Master. Tell me where it is you go during the days."

"Not now. You will learn all you need to when the time is right."

The millions of questions and the lack of answers were driving me mad.

"What…what are you?"

"No more questions, Relone. We need to have a different discussion."

I knew what that meant, and I felt my stomach flip inside me, terrified of the punishment I knew would come.

"Why did you leave here?" His voice was calm, which

only made me more anxious. I could not tell what he was feeling.

"I'm sorry," I muttered.

"Relone…" He paused, sitting on the edge of my bed. "I make these rules not to punish you. I only want to protect you. Do you see why now?"

"I only wanted to make you understand how I feel when you leave me."

"I do, my love."

"I just hate to be alone. I hate being away from you."

"I'm here now."

"Yes, but I'm supposed to be asleep."

He smiled. "Yes. But I will return. I always do."

He kissed my forehead, and sleep washed over me.

"Rest now. I will see you again in the dark hours."

Chapter Four

WHEN I OPENED MY EYES, I saw I wasn't alone. Sophia was right beside me. I brushed my fingers across her cheek. Her skin felt like satin. I pulled the pin from her piled hair, watching the curls fall around her shoulders. When I was with her, all the questions I had and confusion about Verarsoe and the mystery behind his love for me seemed to vanish.

We spent the day lavishing each other with affection.

"Where have you been, Relone?" she asked me softly.

"Away. I was away."

"Where? And why?"

I shook my head, unsure what to say. "I left Master because Master leaves me."

She furrowed her brow and stared deeply into my eyes as if she were trying to read my thoughts. "You confuse me sometimes." She leaned over and planted a soft kiss on my cheek.

She left the room as she always did to do the cooking and cleaning like she was supposed to, and once again, the questions came flooding back—the confusion, the resentment.

Verarsoe's kiss was unlike Sophia's. His was sweet yet bitter. It tasted of life and of power. It was the healing liquid, he told me.

When he did arrive at last, he spoke to me of his absence.

"My dark eyes, do you believe I leave you to hurt you?"

I shook my head. "No. I do not think that, yet I am unsure what I *should* think."

"There is more to your master than you realize," he said. "I leave you to go to others. I cannot tell you everything yet...but in time. I call these others Satan's Own. It is them I leave at night to be with you."

"And I who you leave at day to be with them."

He bowed his head. "I know it doesn't make sense to you right now, but it will."

I felt a sting of betrayal and jealousy. "You are *my* master. You teach me to be a scholar like you. Why do you teach others too? *What* do you teach others?"

"The time will come, Relone. You will know everything in time. Until then, just remember that I love you, and I leave you for purposes that are very important."

"Can you tell me, Master? Why are there not flocks of boys at your doors crying for your magic? If you are such a powerful wizard, a sorcerer, then why are you not being chased after?"

I waited, unsure how he would respond to this, and it worried me greatly.

"Aw, Relone. Do you think for even a moment they are not frightened of me?"

"Frightened?"

"I am a mystery to them, young one—even more than I am to you. They do fear me."

I nodded in understanding, but it was not enough. "Take me with you, Master. Please."

"I cannot, beautiful one. Not yet." He leaned over and kissed my brow. "All in due time."

I wanted to yell out to him as he left my sight. I wanted to demand he answer my questions. Who is Satan's Own? Why do you go to them? What are your secrets, your powers? Please, Master, tell me—tell me everything! I wanted to yell these things out to him, but I didn't. I couldn't. I thought for a fleeting moment about following him, but he would know, and I was not foolish enough to disobey again.

It was all too much for me now. I had to know. I

decided I would do what Verarsoe did. I decided I would sleep during the day and awake at night so I could be with him for as much precious time as possible. Sophia didn't disturb me.

I wondered if others knew the creature that my master was. Did others realize that his life flowed in human blood? If they did, perhaps that is why they feared him.

The candles were lit, and my master was there.

"I see you are not in bed." He smiled at me and sat in the armchair opposite of me.

I was in the parlor with one of my master's tomes. I looked up at him and was relieved to see he did not appear angry.

"No matter," he continued. "I was going to request such a change in your schedule tonight. As it appears you are a day early, we shall begin tonight."

I instantly perked up. "Begin what?"

"It is time I teach you some new things."

I couldn't stop staring through his eyes, trying to decide what to think when he smiled at me that old familiar way. He was like something from a dream or an old fairytale story, and that night, I hoped to taste it again—the "healing liquid."

Chapter Five

MAYBE IT WAS the way he told me that made me second guess him, or maybe it was something deep within myself that told me, but I found myself for the first time, truly frightened of Verarsoe.

"I do not want you to be alarmed," he said. "I am going to show you some magic, child, and I do not want you to be afraid."

Why should I be afraid? I didn't ask him. After all, isn't this what I had wanted? Didn't I want to know his secrets?

He led me to a tavern, the tavern where I had met Claudia. I shied away from the familiar faces of the women. They clung to me and rested upon my shoulders.

"So, this is where you spent most of your time," Verarsoe said with a smile.

I only looked away, staring at the mobs of drunken

fools and the whores clinging to any lovely man who happened to have some time to notice them.

My master didn't seem to notice any of them. He was so emotionless and seemed so cold and vicious. I couldn't understand why. I felt uneasy every time I looked at him.

A fair-haired girl placed a goblet of wine in front of Verarsoe. He smiled but didn't drink it. He stood up from the table.

I heard him whisper again, "Do not be alarmed. Do not weep."

I almost jumped when I heard his voice, as his lips did not move.

Verarsoe approached the young girl. She went completely still, emotionless—unafraid. Verarsoe gripped her yellow hair and pressed his lips to her neck as though to kiss her.

That's when I saw it—his cruel, terrible, animal-like teeth sink into her flesh. Her blood flowed down her neck to her clothing, and Verarsoe swallowed gulp after gulp.

He carelessly dropped the low limp girl on the table. The goblet of ale crashed to the floor. Nobody seemed to take note of it.

He looked into my eyes. "Tell me, my child. Can you endure eternity?"

His lips were stained in blood, and his marble-white face

appeared pink and alive. He lost several of the qualities that made him look like an angel. He looked horrific to me now. Even more so than before. He was no less human than the drunken fools fighting blindly with one another or the whores who clung about me, fondling my hair. He looked so alive; he looked more like he did in my memories than he had ever really been. Not many people had witnessed what Verarsoe had done to the girl, and those who did were either too afraid to question or just far too drunk to take any care in the matter.

"Answer me, child," he pressed.

"I do not know what you wish for me to say, Master." I could hear the terror in my own voice. My master, my *father* was a murderer—a monster of the night, a fiend of legend and myth. One word rang in my mind endlessly. *Blood, blood, and blood.*

"Can you endure eternity?" Verarsoe asked again. He bathed his fingers in the blood that had pooled on the table and held them out to me.

"What are you asking of me?"

"I want you to tell me if you have the heart and stamina for eons of life."

"And why are you asking me this now, Verarsoe? Why at all?"

He sighed. His expression had completely changed as if he wanted me to disregard all I had seen and heard that night. He still looked so human. He looked almost sorrowful—frightened.

"Do you think I would harm you, Relone?"

The words were caught in my throat, mostly because I did not know the answer. I was pulled from my thoughts when I spotted Claudia coming my way. *Oh, good God.* "Come, Master. We can leave now."

For a moment, my mind had completely erased the dead girl, who by then had fallen to the floor. I heard my master whisper my name.

"Don't worry, dark eyes," he said. "If there is a problem, I'll take care of it."

Take care of it? Oh God. Would he kill her too?

He laughed, and it hurt my ears. "Of course not, Relone. No harm will come to her."

I looked at him with surprise, forgetting again that he could read my thoughts. I noticed there was a man following Claudia. I felt relieved to see him, thinking that perhaps she would not take too much of an interest in me, but as she came closer, I saw her lips form the words *I'm sorry.* I didn't know what she meant, but my master was smiling.

The man stepped forward. He was tall, and I had to strain my neck to meet his eyes, which were cobalt blue and made me nervous. His hair was gold, which I found very pleasing to the eye. He was so close to me that I could smell the dust on his clothes. He reached into his pocket and pulled out a pocket watch that dangled on a gold chain, swaying it back and forth in front of my eyes. I gasped, backing away and running into my master. I recognized the watch as my own—or more the one that belonged to my master that I had stolen along with his money the day I ran away. I stood there frozen stiff and trembling. I felt Verarsoe's hand on my shoulder.

"Is there a problem?" Verarsoe asked the man.

"There won't be for long," he answered in a deep, menacing voice.

My master laughed. "What are you saying, Monsieur?"

"That this watch I have belongs to the filthy rodent who stands before you."

"Relone?" He chuckled. "Of course not, sir. You have most definitely made a mistake. My boy here has never before carried such an item as that, nor has he ever seen you before."

"You lie!" the man yelled, alerting a few drunks standing around. "This item was found beneath the blankets of my bed—mine and my *wife's* bed." He glanced at Claudia.

"And how, may I ask, can you be sure that it belongs to Relone and not some other?"

He didn't respond.

"I resent you treating my son like a criminal, sir. I feel it may be wise for you to confront the other men who were lonely while you were away and chose your lovely wife here as their whore."

The man's face twisted in anger, and he swung his fist at Verarsoe. I gasped, shutting my eyes. When I heard a grunt of pain, I opened them to see Verarsoe holding the man's wrist, and he began twisting it until the stranger fell to his knees. Claudia covered her mouth with her hands before crying out, begging Verarsoe to release him.

"It is true, then," the stranger whispered, looking up at my master holding his wrist with his other hand. He stood to his feet. "You *are* a wizard, and that means that your boy here must be one as well."

I smiled, simply because I liked the assumption he had made.

He turned away. "You get away this time," he growled, "but I *will* come back with a way to put an end to your little rodent."

Verarsoe just smiled.

Claudia glanced at me over her shoulder, with the saddest, most guilty look I had ever seen her express.

Verarsoe touched my shoulder, and I sighed.

"Come now, dark eyes," he started softly. "There is something I must tell you now, something I must explain to you."

He took me back home and spoke to me while he

tucked me into bed. "You are young, Relone. When you are older, I want you to leave here."

I felt heat rush to my cheeks, and I clung to his robes. "I cannot leave you ever," I wept. "Please, Master, do not send me away."

"Listen to me, dark eyes. You do not want to be like me."

"Oh, but I do, Master! I do so very, very much!"

"No, Relone. You do not understand."

"I wish to. I have asked, Master. You are a wizard, and I wish to be just like you."

I had already forgotten the fear and revulsion I felt only hours ago at what he had done to the wench at the tavern and Claudia's husband.

"No, dark eyes," he answered. His face was rock hard before he turned away. "Whenever I look at you, your eyes grow tense. Why?"

"Because I feel tense. Because I ache. I ache to know, I ache to understand, and I ache when away from you."

"But if you did understand, you would not wish to be this way."

"But how can I believe such a thing? If I do not understand, I cannot know. I feel as though there is nothing I could want more."

"Then you must answer my question," he whispered. "Can you endure eternity?"

"I still do not understand why you are asking me this."

"Will you be able to live for all time, never grow a day older, and to live the way that I live?"

I was silent for a moment, trying to gather my thoughts, trying to find an answer. "Eternity?" I whispered. "To stay young always—but after death…? I don't understand."

"Listen to me." He placed his cold hands on my shoulders and stared into my tense eyes. "There will be no death."

What are you saying? I knew deep down the meaning of his words, but something inside me did not want to believe it.

"I am saying that you will not die," he answered.

I was startled again by his response to my thoughts.

"Please, Relone, believe me—you do not want this!"

"Why wouldn't I?"

He sighed and turned away again.

"I do not understand why you are asking me to leave, Master."

"It is for your own protection, Relone. You must!"

"I won't," I demanded. "No matter how many times you ask me—I will not!"

"Your life will be misery if you do not listen to me, dark eyes. If you choose to be stubborn, my love, then you can never have peace. I will not let that be your fate. You do *not* want this!"

"I don't believe you."

"I can show you," he said. "Do you wish to know where I go during the day?"

"I do. More than anything."

"Come with me today. I will show you."

I smiled brightly, feeling joy rising within me. I did not dare cry out in excitement, though, because I saw genuine pain in Verarsoe's eyes. Whatever he was going to show me truly hurt him.

At last, I was going to know where my master spent his days without me. At last, I would not be alone. He helped me out of bed and into my cloak.

"It will be light soon," he said. "We haven't much time."

"I will make haste."

He led me far away while it was still very dark and stopped in the middle of a graveyard. Anxiety crept in like it never had before. I knew my master was a wizard. I knew he had powers that could not be explained. It frightened me. In fact, I had never been so horrified in all my life. I felt that with his powers, he could raise the dead—and I feared he would. I stood there, waiting for the shaking in the earth, waiting for the monsters to rise up. Nothing happened.

Verarsoe knelt to the ground and motioned for me to follow. I was trembling, and sweat broke out on my forehead. He did not tell me to not be afraid. I think he wanted me to fear this. He wanted me to believe him about leaving.

He brushed away some loose soil from the ground where I could see what looked to be a wooden door. He lifted it and led me down stone steps to an open room that looked like a cave, only it was not dark and moist. Candle-light flooded the chamber, illuminating what I did not expect to see.

There were beds and hearths that glowed with firelight. There were tables and chairs with shelves of books and tomes. It was just like a manor, only it was smaller, and there were holes in the walls where coffins sat. He told me he had built it himself.

"Come, dark eyes. There is more."

He froze before me, unmoving like a marble statue. I looked into his eyes, but he didn't seem to notice me. He was completely unaware. The stiffness of his features and agelessness of his eyes could have driven me mad had I allowed it.

He blinked then and was looking at me again. I jumped back, still puzzled. I didn't ask him anything because I did not know what to ask. I just waited.

From another part of the cavern emerged others. I clung to Verarsoe's cloak, hiding behind him. At least fifty people stood before me, men and women of all ages—white-skinned like my master, eyes that were strong and fierce. They flashed with an unexplainable power.

I shuddered. The strangers smiled when they caught sight of me, and I gasped when I noticed their canine teeth were pointed, just as Verarsoe's were—pointed like the teeth of wild animals. I stepped back, and they laughed. Verarsoe somehow silenced them.

"If I drink blood as you did at the tavern, what will happen to me?" I whispered, trying to hide the tremor in my words.

More laughter.

"Nothing, my blood child."

"What—what are you?"

"Flesh and blood. I am flesh and blood."

I couldn't respond; I was too confused.

The creatures had not averted their fierce eyes from my face. I wanted to hide behind Verarsoe again, but I had stepped back and was too frightened to move back toward him. As confused as I was, there was an intense fascination and curiosity that consumed me. I only wanted more.

"I want it, Master…to be like you."

"I have broken a rule," he whispered, turning to face me.

I stepped closer to him, no longer afraid.

"I have shown you things and told you secrets you are

not meant to know…unless I planned to kill you—or make you like me."

I almost backed away again but kept my composure. He would not really kill me, would he? He loved me. I wanted to believe that, but it was still in question. Would he let me live now?

"Of course I will let you live," he answered, knowing what I was thinking.

It didn't startle me this time. "Can you make me like you? *Can* you?"

"I can," he answered, "but do you want me to?"

"To never die? What could I want more?"

"Innocence," he declared. "You would want the innocence of mortality, of humanity. Are you certain you can come with me and live off the blood of your kind?"

"I am."

"I only needed you to say it, Relone. I only needed you to be certain. Will you be my companion?"

"I am your companion now."

"Yes, but for how long?"

"Forever."

He smiled. "Yes. Until old age and death consume you —then I will be alone again."

I could see the apparition of myself in his eyes. I could feel strength emanating from him. I had told him this was what I wanted, but I could not shake the feeling that something was wrong. I knew I wasn't dreaming, but at the same time, I couldn't believe it was real. But it was real, and as I felt the gentle press of his teeth in my neck, my fear and confusion grew—to utter horror.

"THE SUN IS COMING," Victor whispered. "Will you continue your story tomorrow?"

"Yes," I answered. "Tomorrow."

Victor smiled as if he wanted to say something more. Instead, he gave me a respectful nod and retreated.

I stopped by the church one last time to say goodnight to Adam. I kissed his cheek, though he didn't feel it. I whispered, "I love you," though he didn't hear it.

I sighed and turned away, trying desperately to break my gaze away from his sweet, sad face. I arrived back home—well, to Adam's house, that is—only minutes before the sun would have burned me away. I gazed at the papers scattered across my desk. I shuffled through all the unfinished manuscripts written by Adam, dozens of stories and beginnings to novels that would never be finished.

A flood of memories raced within me while I tried to sleep that day, and it was a horror film, a gothic tale of terror and pain, but there was also love and comfort. I wasn't sure how this story was going to end. I wasn't sure how much I would tell the young Victor Miller.

Sleep eventually found me, and then the dreams started, and they were beautiful—my beloved master with his burgundy robe, the linens and lace at his cuffs, the black hair tied back with a matching ribbon. I almost wished the times hadn't changed. I wished for the life I once had. I wished my beloved master still lived in the 1300s with me in his underground cave in Paris, France, sheltered from the snow.

Chapter Six

"YOUR STORY IS INCREDIBLE," Victor whispered. "I believe every word of it!"

"You should," I answered with a smile. "There would be no reason for me to lie, now would there? What good would that do either one of us now?"

I continued after a short hesitation, trying to remember where I had left off.

IT WAS the final secret I had been waiting to learn. I begged Verarsoe to tell me as I clung to his cloak with my fingernails.

"Tell me, Master, what is it that you must do? When do you enjoy a meal with me? What in God's name are you?"

"Flesh and blood," he said again. "I swear to you, dark eyes, as I have told you before. I am flesh and blood."

"Flesh and blood?" I echoed. "Please, Master, there is more that you must tell me. I must know what you are. I need to understand how you live and why you hide away in that cave during the day. Tell me why you drank my blood and the blood of that woman at the tavern. And who are those people?"

He sighed. "The final secret, Relone..." He paused. "Those creatures you saw last night are like me, and like me—they are not human."

I felt a sense of surprise, but I realized in that moment that I already knew that much, so I waited for him to continue. I ran my fingers across the shallow wound on my neck.

"I am a blood hunter," he continued. "I live off the blood of the living. The ones I call Satan's Own, they are like me. They are led, guided, and taught by me. Are you ready to join me and live off the blood of humans?"

I couldn't speak now. I was numb. Blood of humans? After all my master had taught me about God and the Bible, I knew it could not be right. I knew he was a monster. He noticed my confusion, my disgust—my fear.

"You do not have to decide right now," he said kindly. "You don't have to decide that for a long time."

I awoke alone, but Sophia came in shortly afterward, smiling.

"My Relone," she whispered. "Your beautiful eyes, why are they always so…tense?"

"I don't know," I answered, turning away.

"Look at me," she whispered.

I turned toward her, smiling then and letting my eyes relax a bit. Her hair was loose, and she brushed her fingers through it and smiled at me.

I twisted a strand of her dark hair between my fingers. I embraced her and felt the warmth and softness in her that Verarsoe did not possess. She was so beautifully…human.

Again, as if it were as normal as anything else, Sophia lay beneath me in all her beauty. It had made me sad to know this would be so brief, so small a time. I didn't want it to end. I wanted to lie that way forever with my beautiful Spanish girl, but that could not happen now.

When I awoke, I was alone, but Sophia had made me breakfast. We weren't so silent anymore; we were more like the closest of companions. Verarsoe knew. I was sure of it. He knew everything, yet he never said a word about it —not until much later.

It was a long time before Verarsoe had spoken of that strange evening. I tried to go on as if nothing had changed, and it was working until the morning that I awoke with the blankets and my body drenched in blood.

I began to scream and bawl, tearing at the sheets in horror, checking my skin to make sure I wasn't the one bleeding. A cold, hard hand covered my mouth; of course, it was only Verarsoe.

"Don't weep, child." He was frightened, looking around as if somebody had broken in.

He released his hand, but I couldn't stop screaming.

"Relone!" he yelled. "Relone!"

The strength in his voice frightened me. I looked at him, quieting my sobbing as best I could. I stared at him and listened hard. I felt no pain. I was too confused and frightened to know if I was hurt.

"They're here, dark eyes," he whispered. "They're here."

"Who?" I yelled. "Verarsoe, who? Are they the ones that you leave me to go to?"

"No. No more questions, Relone. You must be silent if you wish to get out of this. Go wash yourself and get Sophia—quickly now."

I sprang up from my bed and stripped off my stained clothes. I washed the blood off my body, quickly dressed myself, and raced to Sophia's bedroom and woke her immediately.

"Shh," I whispered, signaling her to follow. She grasped my hand, and I led her back to my chambers silently.

"What's going on?" she whispered.

I hushed her. "I don't know."

I stepped into my room to see my master's eyes blazing with some unexplainable fear or confusion. His gaze burned into my eyes, making them fall tense.

"Who are they?" I asked quietly.

"I do not know, but we must get out—now!"

He led us back to his underground cave, and I ached with fear. I saw the confusion pouring out of Sophia as we arrived, but Verarsoe spoke to her softly.

"This is where I go during the day. It's all right. I'll explain everything." He turned to me. "I won't call the others," he whispered, and I felt my body relax.

We stayed there for three days without a single sign that there were others that dwelled anywhere near us. I spent most of my time comforting Sophia, telling her I had been there before and it was safe and that the master was only caring for us like he was supposed to. Every morning when we awoke, there was food waiting for us. I didn't understand why we were hiding, but soon Verarsoe told us.

He said something about evil beings chasing us. We were not even safe in our very own home. Verarsoe was full of dark, vile secrets.

I remember weeping a lot as we stayed in that cave and my master comforting me. I wanted to go home, wanted this to end, all of this horror and pain to end. I wished I could turn back the clock to the day I had left and never do it at all. I didn't want to know his secrets; I wanted to live as I had before—nothing more than a young apprentice with a mysterious teacher. But this was what I had asked for, wasn't it? This was what I had always wanted.

He finally took us back home and explained what had happened.

"It wasn't your blood," he told me. "It was theirs."

"Whose, Verarsoe? Please, Master, you must tell me!"

"I don't know!" he cried. "They're a clan of ancient blood hunters coming after me for something that I carry, something they want."

I clung to his cloak and began to cry. "I cannot endure eternity. I want to leave here as you said."

"It is too late for that now," he said soothingly. "If you do not come with me now, they will destroy you, and whether or not you wish to die, I will not let that happen!"

"It's a sin, sweet Master—a terrible, vile sin."

"Do not insult me, boy! I am what I am, and I cannot change that. I am going to save you."

"Save me?"

"Save you, dark eyes."

My master was keeping something from me, something that he knew, and I should have known. He looked into my tense eyes and studied me for a moment.

"I told you the night would come, and it has."

I was growing impatient for him to confess what he continued to push from his mind. "You seem troubled, Master. What is it?"

"I am going to save you as I said, but before I do, there is something you must know."

I urged him to continue.

"It's about Sophia."

"Sophia?" I yelled. "Is she all right?"

He sensed my terror. "She's all right, Relone."

"Then what is it?"

He sighed again and put his hands on my shoulders. I was terrified now of what he was about to tell me.

"She is going to have a child."

"What?" I yelled. "She cannot be—"

"The child cannot be made one of us. Attempting such would destroy it. It is far too weak a creature."

"So, what do I do?"

"You become like me—and you leave."

"Leave Sophia? For good?"

"Yes."

"No! Verarsoe, I cannot leave Sophia! She's having my child, Master. I cannot abandon them. I love her. Isn't that all right?"

"No," he answered calmly. "No, Relone, it is not all right. Not anymore."

I began to weep openly, not caring what Verarsoe

thought about it. I knew there was no way I could fight Verarsoe. What he wanted was what would be. I tried to think of some way to argue, some way to change his mind. I knew there was nothing—nothing I could do.

Sophia, the Spanish duchess, my love, my chére. I would have to leave her now. I could never be with her again.

I was given one last night, but I was not allowed to touch her after that. It was such a sad thing, that such a night would be so short, so quick, and then—over, never to be spoken of again. As the time passed, her belly had swelled to an enormous size. It was a wonderful thing to love her in such a beautiful state.

The day had finally come—the day for Sophia to have our baby. Truthfully, the very sight of it disgusted me, but she was screaming and weeping, which awoke my compassion as well.

Her hand reached out, grasping at something that wasn't there and squeezing it as tightly as she could. I gave her my hand, feeling her gentle touch that seemed to use all of her strength; she was weakening. I could hardly feel the pressure of her fingers into my own.

I saw the blood come up into her cheeks now, and she looked very flushed and beautiful. Her screaming went on for hours; it was becoming a ghastly sound. I hated it. I wanted her to lie still and quiet. I wanted her to smile at me, but she didn't.

When at last the child was born, Sophia laid her head down upon the bed and let out a long breath that sounded like a sigh of relief, yet the look of pain remained in her expression. I stared at her, but she couldn't smile. The sheets of her bed were drenched in her blood.

I tore my eyes away from Sophia to look upon our child, and I smiled. "Sophia," I whispered. "Darling—we have a daughter."

She smiled thinly, the best that she could.

I smoothed stray wisps of hair off her reddened face. "I love you."

She mumbled something in Spanish, but I do not know what she had said.

We named the baby Belle, meaning beauty, and she truly was a beauty—her small, delicate lips and her tiny voice making sweet mortal sounds. She wasn't crying at all, just slightly squirming when I held her in my arms. Her eyes were black like Sophia's.

This baby was what made Sophia and me one. She was part of me and part of her combined in one beautiful person. I was overcome with a love I had never before felt, even stronger than the love for Sophia or my master.

I took Sophia's hand. "I love you, my little Spanish duchess."

At last she smiled, and it warmed and comforted me. I held the baby wrapped in a thin blanket until she quieted, and I placed her in Sophia's arms. After only a few moments, Sophia whispered something and then closed her eyes to rest as I took Belle back into my arms, smiling down at my precious beauty.

I moved my gaze back to Sophia and took the necklace off her neck and placed it on her head so she looked like a princess. Even as she lay in pain and exhaustion, she looked more beautiful than ever before. I wanted to tell her that, but I didn't. I wanted to tell her that in all of her pain, it only added to the pure perfection of her beauty, that her life showed in her more vibrantly than it ever had before, and it let me realize the true meaning of life. I wanted to tell her that she was an angel to me, who inspired me and drew answers from deep within my soul, answers to questions that the great scientists and philosophers could never even hope to discover. But I didn't. I just watched her breathe as her mind drifted away deep within her dreams.

Verarsoe entered the room. I turned to him, smiling, and he kissed my cheek.

"Belle," I whispered, but he didn't smile.

"Go look at her, dark eyes," he said. "Go on."

I moved closer to her and stroked her hair, trying to ignore the blood-drenched sheets.

"Sophia," I whispered. "Sophia—wake up."

She didn't stir. I handed the whimpering infant to Verarsoe.

"Sophia," I whispered again. I nudged her gently, and her eyes opened. She smiled, and we shared a passionate kiss. I took her hand in mine. Her black eyes closed again, and her hand went limp.

I stroked her hair as I said her name again, but she did not respond.

"I… Sophia…it's getting late. I'm going out with the master. I'll be back soon, all right?"

I felt a cold hand on my shoulder.

"Verarsoe…"

He placed the baby upon her breast. "Come, child," he said softly. "Let them rest together."

"No—Sophia!"

"Relone—"

"No!" I held her hand tighter and began shaking her.

"Relone, please listen to me."

I looked up and stared into his eyes.

"It is better this way."

"Better? What way, Master? What is better?" I refused to believe, refused to admit what I knew was true, that Sophia was dead.

I sank to the ground, weeping bitterly. Verarsoe didn't stop me. I wept until her hand went cold and Belle fell silent and ceased to squirm in her mother's arms.

"Come, child," he whispered. "Your little Spanish duchess is in peace now with your daughter."

"That cannot be!" I cried. "Please, Verarsoe, please do *something*!"

"There is nothing to be done. My condolences."

"But you must! You have magic, Master."

"Dark eyes, you do not understand. I cannot do anything. I have not the capability."

"But how can that be? You are the great Verarsoe Mirior. There must be *something* you can do!"

"There isn't."

I wept for a long time in the arms of my master until I felt sleepy and weak.

"Come now, Relone."

I whispered a prayer, trying desperately to push past the grief that was consuming me.

"No more tears, dark eyes," Verarsoe whispered. "No more tears."

No more tears for my love or my child. They had left me alone with Verarsoe, and my heart was splitting with pain. I wished I could take the clock that held all time and splinter it against the wall. I wanted to stay forever in the comfort of my love and my daughter, in the same room, in the same moment—forever, and I couldn't. The reality of that was excruciating.

I dried my eyes and told Jesus to take good care of them.

"No more tears," Verarsoe whispered again, leaning in closer to me. He repeated those words until it became a meaningless chant.

I could feel his breath upon my neck and the sharp prick of his teeth in my skin. I tensed and let out a strangled gasp. Verarsoe stood over me with my blood still upon his lips. He knelt down and kissed me as a father would kiss a son. He filled my mouth with a thick, hot liquid. I could taste the metal, the iron—blood.

Something in me didn't want it to stop; even as I told myself it was evil, I craved more. I wanted this, didn't I? I was becoming like him—the monster I feared he was.

He drew back. I was crying again.

"No. Master! Do not make me keep your secrets! Do not make me live like a demon!"

But he didn't stop, and I didn't want him to. I wasn't breathing now, but it was all right. I didn't need to breathe. This was everything I needed now. It was as if he were feeding me into another life. He came back to the wound on my neck, and my head spun with dizziness and confusion, but with it was desire and pleasure. He broke the vain in his wrist with his cruel, terrible teeth.

"Drink," he whispered.

His blood poured through me like the sweetest wine. When it was over, I savored the tingling sensation in my body, but it was fading. The pleasure was leaving me, and I cried out to him, begging him not to let the pain come back. It was too late.

I found myself squirming in the sheets of my bed, moaning from the incredible pain in every muscle in my body, screaming louder than I thought possible. It felt as though my body were ripping at the seams and coming apart. Every cell burned.

"Shh," I heard my master whisper. "Let it happen, dark eyes. Let the pain take you where it needs to. It happens with all of us. It's all right, my blood child. It will soon be over. You are giving up all that is human—all but your body and your blood."

It all sounded so magical, so amazing to me. I listened to the melody of his voice, but it was not enough to soothe me. I feared it more than anything, and the pain was unbearable. As I lay there dying, I heard Verarsoe whisper to me to not be afraid. Heavy gasps tore from my chest as I struggled for breath, when just moments before, I hadn't needed to breathe at all. It was as if Verarsoe were breathing for me, but now my lungs struggled for air.

When at last the pain had ended, I was very tired. I sat up in bed and stared into the eyes of my master. I felt no fear now; I felt a new strength, a thickening in my blood and in the surface of my very skin. Yet something felt wrong. My skin was…soft, like silk. There was an odd new sense of strength, of stamina. I felt like nothing could hurt me now. But I was tired, and I wanted to sleep.

"Sleep then, child," Verarsoe whispered. "Dawn is not far. I shall give you one more week in this house. After that, we must burn it, for we are not safe here. You know this. They will come again. We will find a new home until you are ready to join Satan's Own."

I nodded and drifted off to sleep, my master lying beside me as the sun rose.

When I awoke, I couldn't find my master anywhere. I began racing through the rooms, searching for him. I came to Sophia's chambers and found him kneeling beside her bed, stroking her hair. I had never seen him this way before —so weak, so sad.

I touched his shoulder, and when he turned around, I saw that he didn't look so strange anymore—his skin didn't appear white, and his eyes didn't appear fierce. He looked just like a young mortal man.

I realized that as I slept I had forgotten entirely about Sophia and Belle, and now as I stared at them, the facts at last sank into my mind. Sophia and Belle were dead. I couldn't weep for them any longer, but her face wouldn't leave my mind. All I saw was her smiling at me, even as I stood upon the soil where Verarsoe had buried them.

"They do not need to linger in the walls of our catacomb," he had told me. "Those walls are for our victims—here, they will be happy."

I couldn't respond. I could barely listen to Verarsoe. All I could think about was this unbearable thirst, this painful hunger that sent shocks of tingling agony through every limb of my body.

"I know you are hungry, dark eyes. Follow me."

We walked the silent streets of Paris, and my master stopped at a small house. It was cold out; the frost clung to the shingles, and the breeze made the shutters slightly clatter. The night made everything look different to me. The blacks had turned to blues, and the stars shone brightly as if smiling down at me. Verarsoe wrapped his arm around my waist, and up we rose to the rooftop of the house. He signaled silence. I saw his tense eyes staring at the lock inside the window, and instantly it broke apart. I jumped and backed away.

"Shh," he whispered. "Do *not* wake her."

He opened the window and led me quietly into the darkened room. I could see perfectly, every detail of the lovely girl that lay sleeping nestled beneath the blankets.

"Take her," he whispered.

Oh, I wanted her. I really did. Her black hair covered the side of her face as she breathed softly, so warm and comfortable in her bed. I wanted to kiss her on her pink lips and feel warm beneath the blankets beside her. She was so beautiful and innocent.

"Sweet blood lust, Relone," I heard.

Blood lust. Of course. I drank blood now, didn't I? It was blood I was craving. It was blood I wanted. It was not her love I craved; it was her life. As the realization hit me, I knew I had to obey my thirst. I followed my master's movement.

"Closer, dark eyes. Don't be afraid."

I laughed inside myself, loving my newly gained strength. I sank my teeth into the softness of her throat and was filled instantly with pure ecstasy. I tasted salt and metal, all the various flavors of the blood flowing down my throat.

I could see the girl's life through her blood. I saw her loved ones and her desires, her hopes for Heaven, her love for Jesus, and fear of leaving Earth. I could taste the fear she was facing, the fear of not understanding what was being drawn from her body, not understanding what this feeling was.

Blood lust, I whispered through my mind. *Blood lust.*

I took her without guilt, and Verarsoe showed his satisfaction with nothing more than a gentle smile. Now I was his child as I had never been before. I was of his blood now, of his life and his power, and now I was Relone—the immortal child of The King, Verarsoe.

I SPENT one more week in my beautiful home, primarily in my master's bedroom, watching him write whatever it was he was writing. It was in Latin, or maybe it was not, but the language didn't matter, neither did the words. All that mattered was him.

When the week came to a close, I watched in misery as Verarsoe lit the beautiful building ablaze—the home I had known my entire life. I didn't even marvel at the way he did it with nothing more than his dark gift. I was only focused on the fire. The warmth licked at my skin as charred remnants of my childhood fell to the ground at my feet. I turned away, and Verarsoe placed his hand on my shoulder, leading me away, no longer forcing me to endure the sight.

He took me below to our resting place, into the catacombs for our victims. There, the teachings of our kind began, for in this new life of mine, I was not free from the apprenticeship of Verarsoe. In fact, it only meant I was even more a pupil now than I had ever been.

The next night was warm. Everything held some new sense of wonder to me now. Before, my master had seemed cold and white—almost lucent. Now he was warm, with a coloring in his skin I had never seen before. And the blood, oh, yes, the blood, it was like fire through my body. The pounding of the beating heart filled every limb of my new body as I drank. I could feel the warmth of the liquid from the tingling in my fingers to every muscle of my face. Every vessel was filled with this new energy. It could have made me weep, but I wouldn't—not when my master could hear me.

Verarsoe had told me that soon I would hunt in society. That thrilled me more than anything else. I needed sport. I loved the sport, loved playing games with my victims, drawing them into my arms, my embrace, and then…

I deserved the blood of these beauties. That is what my master told me, and I believed him. I believed him because I loved him.

I remember the next night as a night of misery, and I believe this will be painful to tell. I remember Verarsoe asking me if I would come. I told him I would. Of course I would, for I was his child now. Sophia was dead, and without Verarsoe, I had nothing.

He asked me if I would join him and serve the one true master.

"Yes, of course," I answered. "Do I not serve you well?"

"Yes, Relone, you do. But it is not I who is the one true master."

"I don't understand."

"You are a blood hunter now, my child. An immortal

stalker of the night. You are no longer a child of God but of the one that now promises our salvation. If you have visions and wishes of God and of Heaven, you will perish. Lucifer promises our immortality. Without him, we cannot exist."

I took it all in, trying to come to terms with it as best I could, for I could not change it now. I still felt he was wrong. Even though I didn't know many things, I knew that worshiping Satan could not be right. I refused to go with him. I swore to obey and live by God.

My master struck me, and he scorned me, telling me I would burn in Satan's fires and had no reason to have ever been alive.

I didn't want to die; I feared it more than anything. I clung to his velvet, black cloak and sobbed. I choked out between gasps that I would come, that I would come and worship the one true master, serve him as we were meant to. I spoke these words through my blood tears, which truly horrified me.

My master calmed me; he soothed me and told me that everything was going to be all right, and once again, I believed him.

HE LEFT me in his catacomb with the others who were nowhere to be found. It was another terrible night in my memory. I wept for him while he was out on his own. I was alone, and I hated it!

That night, a clan of blood drinkers came to me, woke me from my bed, and demanded I tell them where the "sacred relic" was. I swore to them I didn't know what they spoke of, swore on God and Satan.

They sank their teeth into my neck, beat me, and stabbed me with daggers. The blood flowed out of me, and their eyes became cold as they looked for secrets within it.

For some reason, my wounds were not healing. I thought I was dying; I thought that this is what my master wanted…to kill me.

A loud echo rang from the catacomb, and down the steps fled Verarsoe with anger in his eyes as I had never seen before.

"Get out," he demanded through clenched teeth. "Out." He began screaming as the fury in his eyes grew to fire. "Out! Now!"

My body trembled at the sound of his voice. Where were the others? Why had they not protected me? Why were they hiding from them?

"Get out!" he yelled again. "Get—out!"

All the lamps and mirrors in the room shattered as he

yelled, and their ears bled; mine did too. They raced out of the entrance, covering their ears with their hands.

Another loud echo sounded as the entrance had been shut. My master set me in a soft bed and fed me "the healing liquid." Instantly, my wounds had disappeared, and the pain was gone.

"They will never hurt you again," he said to me. "Oh no, no. Never again will they harm you, my sweet blood child. The others will protect you."

I realized *they* were the ones who had come to me that night. Often times, they would return, scratching at the entrance and babbling nonsense, and my master would run to another room and hold something against his chest. I didn't know what it was that he was protecting. I could only guess it was the sacred relic that the others had been searching for. This went on for years until Verarsoe couldn't take it any longer.

He stormed up the steps and opened the entrance. Down they fled in search of that very same item my master had held against his breast. Only seconds later, they had retreated back up the stairs—in flames. The screams and burning remains of those creatures terrified me, and I wept until my master came to me. He had burned those creatures to dust using nothing but his mind. He scorned me for crying, of course.

"For years, I have protected you! For years, I have

taught you the ways of our kind, and for what? For you to lie here and cry like a child? You are nothing but a coward!"

"Yes!" I yelled between sobs. "Yes, I am a coward."

He sighed and embraced me. More and more these things happened. I wept, and he scorned.

Sometimes he tried to be angry with me, but he just couldn't. I questioned everything he said to me, but he said it was all right to do so, for questions received answers, and therefore helped me learn. I had terrifying thoughts of how I was supposed to live. I realized as I watched my master feed that the girl he had killed in the tavern he had taken carelessly and without caution. He was messy and brutal.

He wanted me to weep; he wanted me to feel pity, but I had not reacted the way he had wanted me to. There was no pity, only fear—fear for me. I tried asking him about God and why we did not worship the Lord. He tried to be angry with me, but I'm not sure if he really was. He told me once again that God condemns us, that God hates us, and that it is Satan who gave us the powers that we possess; it is Satan who promises our salvation if or when we do leave Earth.

I can clearly remember entering my master's domain one evening, and like magic, the torches along the walls were lit as soon as I walked past them. I looked at him with big, almost frightened eyes, but he laughed.

"Power of thought." He chuckled, tapping his finger

against his temple. "You may learn to do the same too, and rather soon I predict."

I marveled at the burning torches, wanting to reach out to them, wanting to touch the flame, for it did not seem real, did not seem natural. I did reach out to it. I could feel the light upon my cheek, feel the heat dripping upon my newborn flesh. I pulled my hand away before touching the flame, remembering that it was the only thing that really could hurt me.

I heard Verarsoe laugh under his breath so softly I probably wouldn't have been able to hear it if I were mortal.

"Why do you laugh?" I questioned. "Are you angry? Are you pleased?"

He laughed again. "Neither, dark eyes. You just make me laugh sometimes."

I didn't respond, only looked around at the little cave-like place we were in. Verarsoe called it a catacomb, and so it was— after all, the walls held coffins, coffins of only the most beautiful and adored victims. I was hungry again, and Verarsoe wanted to take me out. Verarsoe Mirior the sorcerer—he was so fascinating to me. And he did take me out; he took me back to my little tavern, the one where I had met Miss La Croux, if you remember.

He told me that I must always dispose of the bodies, for dead bodies around these parts were not simply something that came about every day.

"If you find them beautiful, dark eyes, and if you love them, you may take them back to our secret home, and there you can keep them forever."

"And what use, Master, would I have for them there?"

"Perhaps none. But it is what some of us like to do. There are creatures who do things differently. There are creatures who hate that they are immortal, and they roam the world in misery, looking for a way out of their terrifying existence. Most of them eventually cast themselves into the fire or the light of the sun."

"Why?" I yelled in shock. "Why, sweet Master, is it possible to hate the power and protection of this life?"

"Now, don't you go getting too far ahead of yourself, boy." The word *boy* was cut short by his laughter. "You may decide sometime soon that perhaps this life is not at all what you wish for or what you desire at all."

"I live it now!" I told him. "I love that I can speed past mortals like a quick shadow. I love that I can read their words before they speak them. I love that nothing can hurt me. I love that I am immortal, Master! I love that I am a blood hunter—and I really love—blood!"

"Of course you do." He laughed. "Of course you do."

"I love being so superior to humans."

"Superior to humans? Where did you get an idea like that?"

"Well, are we not?"

"In a sense, Relone. I just want you to realize that you are more human than anything else."

"Am I now, Master?"

"Of course, dark eyes. Of course!"

"Please explain."

He sighed. "Too many questions but if you must know—do you not have a human heart, my love? A human body?"

"I do."

"You have a human heart, human blood, and a human body. You are more human than you are monster. I want you to remember that."

"Are you angry with me, sir?"

He laughed under his breath. "I try to be, Relone—I try to be."

I smiled. He did try, but his love for me made it nearly impossible. I was literally of his blood now, and the words "blood child" came more often than they had when I was a young mortal boy.

"I respect your optimistic views on your new life," he had told me, "but is there no pain?"

"There is pain, Master, and there is grief. I can feel it if I want to, for it is there. But I do not. I do not feel it because I do not want to. I push it aside as you had said I must, for I cannot help that I have to kill."

"That you cannot," he answered. "I am pleased you realize it. What have you learned, Relone?"

"That life is worth embracing, no matter how much of it you may have left."

"Yes."

"And that even though we kill, we must respect them."

"Yes."

"You are a great teacher."

"I am glad you think so. Now, write me a paper on what we just discussed."

I laughed until I realized he wasn't smiling, that he was serious. So, I groaned and got straight to work, mentioning that I knew I had much to learn and that I, as a blood hunter, needed more knowledge than I would as a mortal boy. I flattered my master, complimented teachers throughout my project, and he was rather pleased with my finished results.

"Yes, Master. I am now a scholar like you."

"Almost." He laughed. "Don't get ahead of yourself. I do not wish for you to become a scholar like me as much as I want you to become an immortal like me. You will become an immortal like me, will you not?"

"Oh, I will, Master!"

He kissed my hair. It was the perfect time, and he embraced me, chuckling quietly to himself. "Oh, Relone. You truly are a delight!"

Chapter Seven

THE NEXT EVENING, Verarsoe took me back to that tavern to feed. He hoped I would see Claudia—I hoped differently. I scanned the place but witnessed only drunken fighting and loud, profane laughter. I was glad I did not see Claudia, but then emerging from a crowd, came lovely Miss La Croux. I wasn't sure if she had seen me, so I turned my face, shying away behind Verarsoe. Of course, how many other boys around have gray, silken waves of hair and are escorted by the richest and most feared man in Paris?

"Master, let's leave," I said, turning away.

He grabbed me by the hood of my green cloak and pulled me back to him. "Oh, no you don't," he snapped, and he growled through clenched teeth, "Don't… be…obvious."

He told me I couldn't let anybody know the creature that I was, that the knowledge would earn them a death sentence. I groaned and looked right at her.

"Relone!" she cried in her silvery voice, rushing over to me.

Verarsoe smiled and tapped his finger against his temple.

"Stop it," I whispered, nudging him with my elbow. "I will not invade her mind."

She looked so human now; I could see the blood in her cheeks and the life under her flesh. I could hear her blood rushing through her body like the sound of river water. Her dark hair rested in tight ringlets down her shoulders, and she was suddenly fascinating to me, a different creature entirely unto herself!

"Mademoiselle La Croux," I said, trying to sound pleased to see her. "Stop it!" I whispered again to Verarsoe.

Read her thoughts, he was saying. I refused. It was the worst invasion of human privacy, and even without me going into her mind, I knew what she wanted. I knew she wanted me to kiss her. She put her soft, warm, milky arms around my neck. I didn't want to kiss her for fear of her feeling my fangs. But my master looked at me harshly, and his eyes flashed with a frightening kind of strength...or power. I leaned in toward her, and our lips met. I am sure she felt the press of my fangs into her lip, but she ignored.

Verarsoe tapped his finger against his temple again, but he wasn't smiling; he was angry.

I shrugged Claudia away. "I have to go."

"Relone!" my master yelled as I hurried toward the door.

I heard Claudia calling my name, asking what was wrong. I quickly left the tavern, but she followed. I can remember actually pushing her away, yelling at her to get away from me. I think she was crying. Was she in love with me?

"Please," I yelled. "Leave me." I didn't completely understand my full strength yet, and when I pushed her the second time, she had fallen.

I raced home and closed myself in my bedroom. I was angry and embarrassed. When we returned to the catacomb, I threw myself forward onto my bed and refused to move.

Verarsoe stormed into my chambers. "You are going back to that tavern tomorrow, aren't you?"

"No!" I yelled. "I will not!"

He left the room. I thought he was going to leave me in peace, but I was wrong. My master returned only moments later, standing behind me. I knew he was there, but I pretended not to notice.

It was then I heard his whip crack, and a sharp pain erupted across the backs of my legs. I growled in anger and rolled over and sat up. He struck my thighs until I screamed. The wounds healed instantly, but each blow sent a sudden pain through my skin. I stood up, and with a cry of fury, I hurled myself toward him. He grasped me by both my shoulders and threw me down upon my bed where I hit the headboard hard.

"You get up, boy!" he yelled. "You will go back to that tavern tomorrow. Do you hear me?"

"You cannot tell me what to do anymore, Verarsoe!"

"You may be immortal, but you are a boy, no bigger than that. Where do you think you are going to go if not with me?"

I turned away.

"You look at me, boy! And wipe that scowl off your face before I whip you again."

I ignored.

He came over to me and stood by the side of my bed and pulled me down by my arm. He pulled me through the house as I kicked and screamed and led me to the room we would call the guest room in modern time. It was much like the room in the old manor he put me when I was a mortal boy and didn't deserve dinner, but Sophia had always let me out after he had left. This time, I had no way out. He threw me in and locked the door. I screamed, banging on the door with my fists. I hadn't fed yet that night and had no strength left in me. Even if I could have broken the door, I was too weak.

I started to cry when I heard him leave. I didn't understand how he could refer to me as his sweet, beloved blood child one moment and treat me like a misbehaving child the next. Did he love me or not? He left to the others I am sure, Satan's Own, and I cried myself to sleep.

When I awoke, I was in my master's bed. He was standing beside me, and I covered myself with my arms as if protecting myself from a blow.

"Don't cower, Relone," he said. "I am not going to strike you again. Look at me."

I looked up at him and held out my arms. He embraced me, and I hugged him around his shoulders.

"I will not say that I should not have struck you, but I am sorry I let you go hungry."

I watched as he unbuttoned his white shirt, revealing his beautiful, shimmering skin. He slashed his naked chest with his fingernails and put his hand on the back of my head. He pushed me toward the wound. His blood was hot and tasted spiked with power. I was drunk off his blood, and I continued to widen the wound with my teeth until it was too large to fit my mouth around. I had no more hunger left in me, no more pain, but I couldn't stop. I couldn't get enough. I drank and drank until he pushed me away.

"You will go see Mademoiselle La Croux," he started. "Won't you, Relone?"

"Yes, *Master*. I will, Master."

He smiled and embraced me again. I rested my head against his chest, realizing the wound was no longer there.

We found Claudia at the tavern that night, and she took us back to her house. Verarsoe apologized for my behavior and for what he had done to her husband. He told her that I didn't know what I was saying, He said I hadn't been feeling well and that I was all right now and more than ready to visit with her.

"He was begging me to let him go back out that night," he said, laughing.

She laughed too, and I tried my best to act amused and embarrassed.

"I told him it was too late and that he needed to rest. He kept insisting until he fell asleep."

"Oh, such a sweet boy." She chuckled, looking at me.

Claudia and I spent most of the evening talking, but Verarsoe, more than I did, ended up with his shoulders and face covered in kisses. It was nothing to either one of us. He did it to punish me for disobeying him—and it worked. She was human, simple as that, weak and dirty. At the same time I found her beautiful and fascinating, she also made me sick.

I hated it. I hated being around her. I was haunted by memories of the love we had shared in her bedroom when I had been mortal, and that made me even sicker.

I was allowed to go home when I chose, and my master

told me I could rest early that night if I wanted, that we would not go to the others that night. I didn't understand.

"But, Master, what about where we had left off in my teachings? What about the works of Aristotle and Plato? What about the teachings of God? Why so suddenly, Master, has God completely vanished from within you?"

"Do not speak of God!" he yelled, pointing an angry finger at my chest. "Why should I teach you about such things? Why must I teach you about human ways, human history, and human government? Why?"

I didn't answer.

"No, my blood child, you needn't know those things. I will teach you all that is important. I will teach you how to be the strong immortal that I have made you to become."

I only nodded, unable to protest.

The next evening, another dreadful thing happened. More strangers had come to our secret domain. It wasn't a clan of ancient blood drinkers in search of my master's writing. It was more than that. As I sat remembering my life and mourning over all I had lost, I was grabbed from behind, my mouth and eyes covered. The hands were cold and hard like my master's. I was completely terrified. I felt as if the dead blood in my veins had come back to life, and my cheeks felt flushed. I struggled as another stranger wrapped their arms around my waist. I tried to scream, but my voice was caught in my throat. I reached back, clawing at their hands and wrists, squirming and writhing, but it was useless. Their strength was incredible; it was the comparison between Verarsoe and me as a mortal boy.

They dragged me silently through the catacomb until I could hear the rush of the wind in my ears. At least five strangers held me as I wept. I wept for my master and for myself. I wept because I thought that now, it was truly the end. They were calling me by a familiar name. I continuously heard the name *Cassiodorus*, which from my master's teachings, I had come to know as a Roman aristocrat who rose to a high rank in Theodoric's government. A man of strong Christian beliefs, he was a teacher of Christian faith. Why on earth would they call *me*, a satanic immortal, by the name of a respected Italian Christian? I had read Cassiodorus' book, *Introduction to Divine Human Readings,* more than once, and I knew that this man had nothing to do with me.

"Our Cassiodorus," they continued to whisper.

Dawn crept near. I could feel it, and in the arms of these strangers, I fell asleep. When I awoke, I was surrounded by a flock of blood drinkers, some cloaked and hooded in black, others dressed as I was dressed.

"Cassiodorus," they said.

A man with auburn hair stepped forward. He was small in build and only a bit taller than me; he appeared to have been grown when he was made, with his beard clean-shaven and his hair clipped to a lovely length upon his shoulders. He stared at me, waiting a moment before speaking.

"You are the pupil of the evil, satanic Verarsoe," he said.

No response.

"Will you serve Satan, Cassiodorus?"

Although he had not called me by my name, I had no doubt he was speaking to me. I just didn't know why.

"Should I not?" I answered.

"Christ is the Lord, Cassiodorus. You know this. You have a religious soul. Why do you let Verarsoe take that away from you?"

"It's what I was taught."

"You are a believer in God," he exclaimed. "Your heart is full of more goodness and more faith and knowledge in God than anybody we have found. We want you, young one, to be the leader, the leader of this leaderless group."

"Are you not the leader?"

He laughed almost silently. "I am not. Our leader is dead."

I did not ask how or why to any of this yet. I was confused, and I was frightened as well. I wanted to go home. I wanted to be enclosed in the arms of my master and hear him tell me that everything would be all right.

"Cassiodorus was a Christian man, who led a monastic school in Italy," he said.

"As I know."

"He led the teachings of Christ and of the Bible."

"Also, as I know. But I must ask you before any more is said, can you tell me where I am?"

"Eze," the stranger answered, "in Southern France. Is it not beautiful?"

"It's difficult to say," I answered, "being in a place such as this."

"The catacomb?" He laughed brightly. "Where else is there to stay?"

"Why Cassiodorus? Why not somebody other than him, and why *me* as Cassiodorus?"

"Our former master taught us the ways of Cassiodorus," the auburn-haired immortal said. "He told us that he was an honorable man. Our master had an intense love for this man. He knew him as a mortal and honored his ways. Of course, being mortal, Cassiodorus eventually perished, and our leader wanted to continue honoring him. He said he was *our* Cassiodorus. But he is dead now, and we are alone."

"Why do you live beneath the ground like Satan when you don't wish to serve him? Why do you live like him? There are other places to stay sheltered from the light."

"I see you have much to learn. But so do we. Can you not teach us the ways of the Lord?"

"The Lord hates us!" I said. "He condemns us for what we do. The Lord promises us nothing. We are evil, whether we want to be or not."

"But how can you say this?" he argued. "Why should we not worship and love the Lord simply because he hates *us*?"

"For that very reason. Why would you waste yourself, loving and worshipping him, when all he does is condemn you? Our one true master is the one who promises us power, and in the feed, he promises us pleasure. Our one true master is Satan."

"But how can you believe that?" he yelled. "Was it not God who gave us our lives?"

"Of course not!" I yelled. "God gave us our mortal lives, but our human souls are dead now, and our evil souls have been born. Satan gave us our immortal lives—he did."

"I know you do not believe that, Cassiodorus. We looked into your mind and into your heart, and we know what you truly believe. We have to have you, simple as that. Stop acting, Cassiodorus."

"Your former master, who was he? And if I may ask—how did he die?"

"His name was Ashman," he answered. "An ancient

one from the ancient world, born to darkness some five-thousand years before the birth of Christ."

"And why Cassiodorus?"

"Cassiodorus was a mortal companion of Ashman, as I have told you. He admired Cassiodorus for his faith and purity. He admired what he did in his teachings of the ways of the Lord. After his death, Ashman took on his ways, enlightening his kind on the teachings of the honorable Cassiodorus."

"And his death?"

"Came later than expected," he answered. "He told us he was the oldest living immortal and that the world had changed, changed too much for him to go on." He sank his head low as he continued. "He cast himself into the fire of his death. He is gone now, but before he died, he had told us to find the child of the evil Verarsoe Mirior."

"My master is no more evil than any of us here. I do not see why you think I could teach you what Ashman could not."

"It is not that he couldn't teach us. It is that he hadn't the time, Cassiodorus. He hadn't the time to teach us all we needed to know. He said that his time had ended and that he had put it off for far too long, so he left us with you to finish our teachings."

"With me?"

He nodded.

"But what do I know of you? How do I know that I will want to stay with you?"

"I cannot guarantee that, Cassiodorus," he answered calmly. "But will you not even try?"

I didn't want to answer. I was frightened of him—of his age. I couldn't answer, so I changed the subject. "I don't like you. You're Greek, and to me, no Greek belongs in France."

He wasn't angry. He laughed. "The Greeks did not come here as conquerors. They came here as settlers—settlers of Marseilles."

I sighed.

"We Greeks came here from the island of Rhodes, the first of us around 650 B.C."

"And I suppose you have a lovely story to tell about the founding of Marseilles."

"I do." He chuckled. "There is a story of a lady of Ephesus, called Aristarchê, who said she had dreamed of the goddess Artemis. In this dream, Artemis had told her to take one of the statues that was sacred to her and join with the Phocaens, under their captain, Simos, and his son, Protis. They were merchants. She was told to sail with them to the new land. Aristarchê found these merchants immediately and told them of her dream. She went with them into the west with the sacred statue of Artemis. As they sailed, they eventually discovered a bay, a bay that not many could find. Within the bay was a perfect harbor, large enough for dozens of ships, but the place was mysteriously vacant and quiet. They docked and went up into the hills. There, they found that the Ligurian king, Nannos, had already discovered the land. King Nannos was, at the time, trying to arrange a marriage for his beautiful daughter, Gyptis. All great rulers would be invited to a feast, where Gyptis would choose a suitor whom she found most pleasing to her. Since the Phocaens were considered honorable, they were invited to the feast. When Gyptis entered the room where the men were feasting, she held a goblet of pure water, which she would give to her chosen suitor. She went straight to Protis. Protis drank the pure water, and King Nannos rejoiced saying it was done by the gods.

"Protis and Gyptis were married and were given the harbor of Massalia, which is now Marseilles. Protis changed his name to Euxinos, meaning *the honored guest,* and in return, Gyptis changed her name to Aristoxena, meaning *the best of guests*, since she was of royal blood. She became co-ruler with her husband of the harbor, and because Artemis was the guardian goddess of the land and directed the Greeks on their journey into the west, that entire part of Southern France was handed over to her.

"All this had come to pass because Aristarchê, the lady of Ephesus had dreamed of Artemis. Therefore, she too was given a position. She became priestess of the shrine of

Artemis built overlooking the harbor. The statue brought from Greece was placed in the sacred precincts. Aristarchê to this day is an honorable woman in the hearts of the Greeks. This story is told to every generation."

I suppose I had no doubt to believe that this story was true or at least based off some kind of truth, and because of the passion in which this man had told his story, I couldn't avert my eyes from his face. I liked this man. Greek or not, I liked him. I didn't want him to know this, but I am sure he did. Even though I liked him, would I still want his coven to obey me as their master? Yes, it had always been a dream of mine to be my own master, to not have to obey Verarsoe as my leader but to have others obey me as theirs. What would it be like to teach these people of the Lord? A saint of evil—that's what I saw myself as, a saint of evil. But this man was right. I did have a religious soul, I did believe in the ways of God and of Christ, and I did want to teach these things to as many as possible, especially our kind. The love for God overflowed in my body. All the feelings that I had constantly pushed aside to please my master came flooding back through my limbs. Jesus was alive in my blood, and I could hear the words of God in my mind, and I smiled.

Chapter Eight

THE LESSONS of the Lord needed to be taught to these creatures. I would be as Cassiodorus, the way he had constructed a school solely for the teachings of Christ. I would be their leader. But what about Verarsoe? He could find me no matter where I was, couldn't he? I saw this as a true test of his love for me—one, unfortunately, he had failed.

Immediately following my decision to lead this coven, the auburn-haired one approached me with a chalice. Most likely Greek, it was bronze and sculpted with winged horses and intricate designs. Within the chalice were three drops of blood from each of the coven members, mingled with my own. They were chanting Latin words, but I didn't listen. I knew they had said "Hail Cassiodorus," and other things relating to their devotion to me.

At the end of their chant, I drank from the chalice, savoring each individual taste, easily being able to tell what blood came from what body. All of these creatures were old and all of them strong. Yes—Hail Cassiodorus, the pupil who has become the teacher.

VICTOR STARED, wide-eyed, entranced by the story.

"I was angry during those times. Lead the coven I did, and teach them I also did, but I was miserable and very alone. Even before my auburn-haired companion, Cintle, had left the world as Ashman had, I was alone. I was often confronted by one of the members, a Russian—Alexander. He always believed that Ashman was alive, and that only added to my frustration with life. Blood was the only comfort and pleasure I could find. For two hundred years, I led this coven, and I grew stronger as the years passed until my physical strength was beyond any of the members of my coven, and yes, they obeyed me as much as they feared me.

"Also, as time passed, my grief consumed me, and I refused to enter the places of the Lord. Everything that I knew of God and of Christ had left me, and I didn't dare even enter the smallest of churches. With the death of my faith came the death of my coven. I don't like talking about the ending of my coven. It is painful and regretful, and I refuse to speak of it. I have already gone off and told you too much already, but I cannot change that now. It was the year 1600 before I was back in Paris, searching for Verarsoe. I never found him, nor did he find me. I traveled across the world until finally, I came to the place where I found you.

"You remember, don't you, Victor? The love we used to share. Do you remember?"

"Yes, I remember. I remember everything you have taught me. I remember all the pain of losing my family and my child. I remember it all—and I remember Daniel. There is one thing you have not yet mentioned."

"What would that be, Victor?"

"The Book of Shadows. Did you not say you knew all the secrets of The Father?"

"I learned of these things from my beloved Cintle. He was a favorite of Ashman when he led the group, and Cintle knew his story. Ashman the Great was his name, an Egyptian Pharaoh of the ancient world. He was created by Ké Hé Zule himself and so knew all there was to know of the legends. If The Book of Shadows even still existed, I didn't know, and I didn't care. Of course, we know now that the book is the most sacred of vampiric possessions."

"So, you have never read the book?"

"I haven't," I said, smiling. "But I know the stories, and

I know the legends. And my very last confession to you, Victor, is that I do love you. My confession is that I never stopped loving you to begin with."

He smiled, and we shared a warm embrace.

"May I ask something of you, my old friend?" he asked softly.

At last—that was the Victor I knew and loved so well, so long ago. "I would like you to," I answered.

"The end of your coven… I mean not to cause you pain, Relone, and I know it may be painful for you to speak of—"

I put my hand up and sighed. "I understand. There really isn't a way for me to tell you. My story was painful enough as it was—painful and sore.

"I loved those beautiful creatures. They were my angels. I grew to love them all as much as I had loved my master, but times change, dear Victor, as we do not. Many of our kind do not have the will to go on. Their time had ended, and mine did not. Some had died as Ashman and Cintle had died. Others simply disappeared somewhere far from France. My time had not ended yet. Mine will go on for I don't know how long. I wanted to stay here as long as I could, and when I began feeling that despair, when the thoughts of ending my time came to mind, I needed somebody to save me. I wanted that somebody to be you, but it wasn't."

"It couldn't have been."

"I know. It was Adam. I know that now. I followed him for months after I met you, and I found out that was all I ever needed. All I ever really wanted was a pupil like I was to Verarsoe, somebody who would look up to me and love me, and fortunately, that is what I found in Adam."

I couldn't say any more. This is all there really was to it. I was hungry, and the night was waiting for me. I loved to feed, loved the sport, and Adam would soon learn that he loved it too.

Victor didn't say much in response. All I could think about that morning was my master and how lucky I had been that The Book of Shadows had been found. The immortal known as Josh Coville was a fool, publishing the book into mortal bookstores. The book was fortunately placed under fiction, and Verarsoe had sent out creatures of our kind to burn any bookstore that held it and steal every book that had been purchased. The lone remaining copy of The Book of Shadows is the original, held safely and secretly by Verarsoe only.

And so, my tale does end here. Things that followed in my later years had caused me to change in many ways. When I first met Adam, I knew he was the one that Cintle had told me about, the one that Ashman said would someday be chosen to lead the new era. How I knew for certain it was this particular era, I cannot tell. All I know is that if Victor would not have turned him—I would have.

As my understanding of Adam grew, my love for him grew as well. The night in the graveyard when I destroyed the beautiful girl with the golden hair, the night I justified the murdering of Adam's wife, that was the night he taught me something, and because of this beautiful thing he taught me, he taught all our kind. Do not kill the innocent. Kill the killers; kill the sinners. Feed off the blood of the evildoer or those who are in pain. Those victims are the ones that are meant for us.

MY CHILD WOULDN'T MOVE. He hadn't fed in months. I felt as though I hardly knew him anymore. I knew nothing of these years he had been gone, the ones he has not told a soul about. Rayne had at last returned home, and all seemed so good now, but nobody could wake my Adam, not even his love.

There was no telling how long he would remain.

About the Author

Sara J Bernhardt is an author and poet who has been writing since a very young age and is a winner of several poetry and short story contests. It is clear that Bernhardt writes in a realistic tone while still creating the enthralling feeling of fantasy. Her writing puts readers in a world that they will truly love to be a part of. Though the writing is edgy and catching it is also not too complex which makes it a comfortable and enjoyable read for everyone.

You can follow Sara at these locations:

Facebook:
www.facebook.com/Sara-J-Bernhardt
Website
www.sjbernhardt.com

Other Works by Sara J. Bernhardt

Summer's Deceit (Hunters Trilogy – Book 1): Jane Callahan is a reclusive, seventeen-year-old high school student dealing with the death of her beloved brother. Her home in Southern California with her mother is a constant reminder of her loss and pain. In hopes of escaping her past she moves to North Bend Oregon to live with her father, where she meets a beautiful boy named Aidan Summers. Jane is intrigued by his looks as well as his unusual ways of attempting to get her attention. After months of uncommon conversation and frustration, an uncertain romance brews between Jane and Aidan, but Aidan has a ghastly secret that could destroy everything.

https://books2read.com/SummersDeceit

Summer's Shadow (Hunters Trilogy – Book 2): Aidan Summers, a seventeen-year-old, stunningly beautiful genius, somehow finds his way into the life of Jane Callahan; a lovely girl trapped in soggy North Bend, Oregon. In this new Tale by Sara J. Bernhardt, Aidan relates his side of the story. All of his dark secrets are revealed and all of his motivations behind his strange ways become known as the story unravels in a captivating narrative of suspense, romance, courage...and murder.

https://books2read.com/SummersShadow

Summer's Redemption (Hunters Trilogy – Book 3): The secret alliance of The Silver Wing and the waging war with their evil rival, The Sevren, come into full view in a new light. The evil that still lurks and stirs behind the supposed destruction of The Sevren steps out of the shadows and spins a new tale of adventure, suspense, romance, mystery and terror.

https://books2read.com/SummersRedemption

Behind Blue Eyes Series

Adam Gold – Book 1: Fleeing the French invasion of Geneva Switzerland in the 1700s, Adam Gold books passage to America with his family. On the ship, Adam's daughter falls fatally ill. A mysterious man comes to Adam with a way to save his child by turning Adam into something darker than human.

https://books2read.com/AdamGold

The Medallion – Book 2: Adam Gold, an immortal with sweet eyes of blue, rushes through the centuries on a quest for reason and a thirst for revenge. To cope with his pain and regret, he sleeps away the years and awakes in a new era with a powerful, ancient vampire who sets her sights on him.

https://books2read.com/Medallion

Golden Shackles – Book 3: When the ancient queen, Sekhmet snatches up Adam, he is faced with a terrifying decision. To help aid her in her vile plans or dare to stand against her.

https://books2read.com/GoldenShackles

Plus 3 more segments!

In Gray

After a near fatal car crash brings Daisy Carmichael the ability to see the future, she is plagued by not only the things she sees, but the deadly secrets of the boy who saved her life.

https://books2read.com/InGray

Harvest Moon

Adeline Blackwood is a supernaturally gifted noble young woman who will do whatever is necessary to

be with the man she loves.

https://books2read.com/HarvestMoonBernhardt

Also from the Lavish family

The Norn Novellas

A. Nicky Hjort

https://www.lavishpublishing.com/authors/nicky-hjort-1/

The Norn Novellas are all chapters in the epic saga of the youngest and most fickle of the four Norn Sisters. The same feisty immortal creature who must escape her inherent inner darkness to learn the meaning of life.

Between the Trees

Kathy Moczerniak

https://www.lavishpublishing.com/authors/kathy-moczerniak/

A beautiful coming of age with a dark side that one teenager must fight to overcome…

Beyond Kathryn Lucas' first memory of her father's tree lay a dysfunctional path of violence, heartbreak, and secrets within a family severely entrenched in the vicious cycle of abuse. A lifetime of fear drives her from her home, and the teenage girl finds refuge with an aunt and uncle determined to protect their niece.

Distressing flashbacks unravel in Kathryn's fragile mind among the turmoil encircling her as she struggles through adolescence and descends into her pain-ridden past. When the summation of her unsettling memories allows the darkness to overtake her, she becomes desperate to unearth the light.

Inspired by a true story, Kathryn must hold on tightly to those who love her, searching for her place in a world threatening to break her as she fights to overcome life's betrayals before she is deprived of her future.